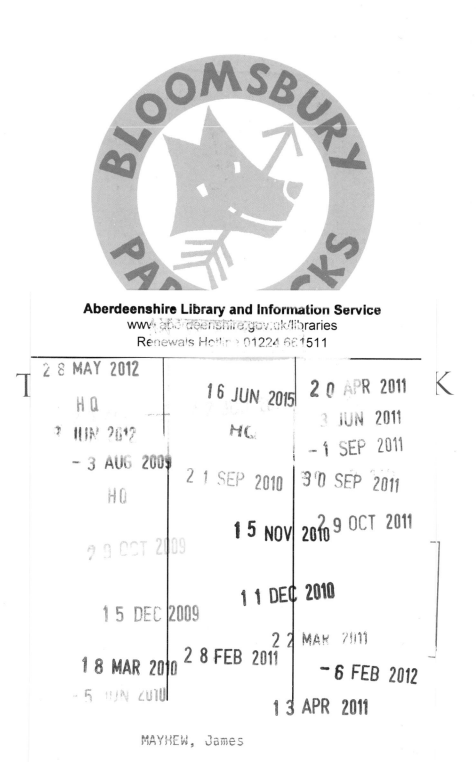

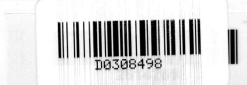

For Gabriel, who gives the best cuddles - J.M.

For Maxwell & Yvonne - S.H.

First published in Great Britain in 2008 by Bloomsbury Publishing Plc
36 Soho Square, London, W1D 3QY

A CIP catalogue record of this book is available from the British Library

ISBN 978 0 7475 8759 0

Printed in China

1 3 5 7 9 10 8 6 4 2

FSC Mixed Sources
Product group from well-managed forests, and other controlled sources
www.fsc.org Cert no. SCS-COC-00927
© 1996 Forest Stewardship Council

Where's My Cuddle?

James Mayhew

Illustrated by

Sue Hellard

BLOOMSBURY CHILDREN'S BOOKS

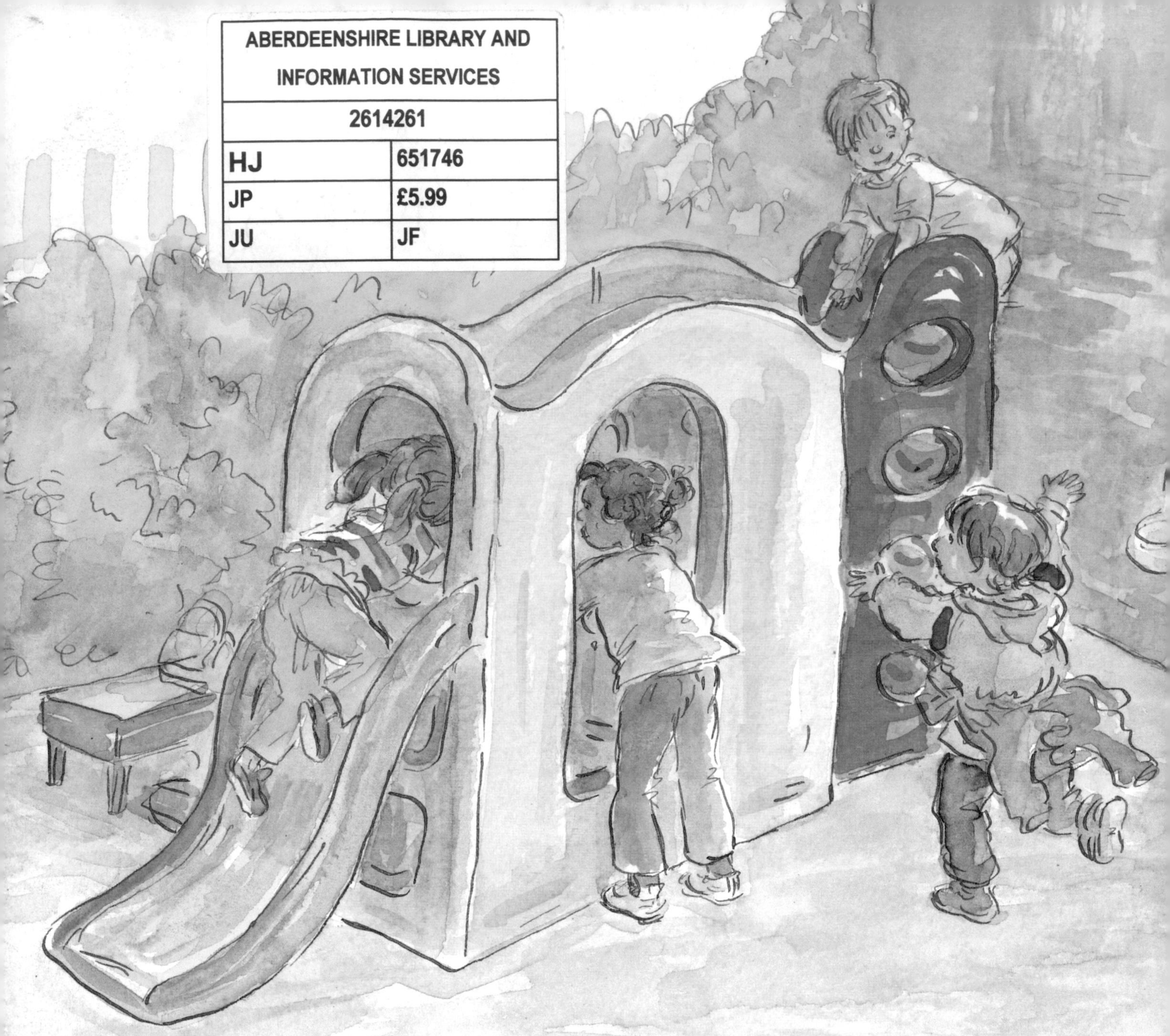

Jake said goodbye at the school door.

'Come and have a cuddle,' said Mum.

'MUM!' said Jake. 'I don't want a cuddle.
Everyone will think I'm a baby.'

And Jake ran off to play.

But at the end of the day, things hadn't all gone Jake's way. And he was heard to say,

'Where's my cuddle?'

'You said you didn't want it,
so I gave it to Dad,' said Mum.

So Jake said to Dad,

'Where's my cuddle?'

'I gave it to the cat,' said Dad.

Jake went to the cat.

'Where's my cuddle?'

he said.

'I gave it to a witch,' she said,
'because she gave me a nice fish.'

Jake went to the witch and said,

'Where's my cuddle?'

'I've given it to a wizard,' said the witch,
'because his spell went wrong.'

So Jake went to the wizard.

'Where's my cuddle?'

he said.

'Goodness!' said the wizard.
'I gave it to a knight in armour
who was off to see a dragon.'

Jake found the knight.

'Where's my cuddle?'

said Jake.

'I gave it to
the princess,'
said the knight.

Jake went over to the princess.

'Where's my cuddle?'

‘It was a good cuddle and it made me brave,’ said the princess, ‘so I gave it to the dragon and tamed him with it.’

Jake said to the dragon,

'Give me my cuddle!'

'That's no way to ask,' said the dragon.

'Can I have my cuddle, PLEASE?' said Jake.

And the dragon
gave him a cuddle.

Jake rode home with the knight and the princess and the dragon, just in time for tea.

And after tea Mum put him to bed and said,
'Now where's MY cuddle, please?'

'Well,' said Jake, 'I want to keep it!'

'What if I give you another one?' said Mum,
cuddling Jake.

'Then I'll give you this one,' said Jake.
'But be careful who you give it to.'

Enjoy more fantastic Bloomsbury picture books . . .

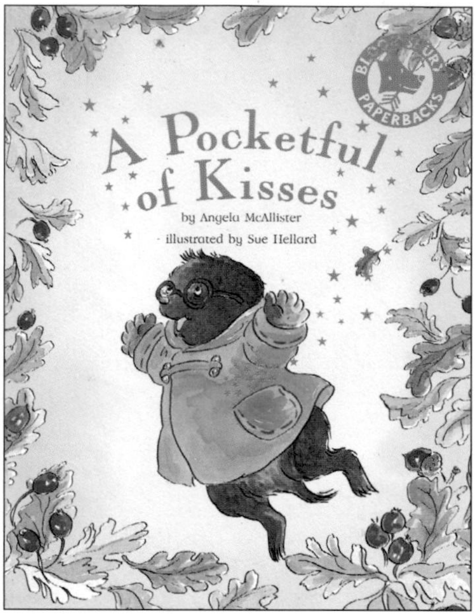

A Pocketful of Kisses
by Angela McAllister
& Sue Hellard

Milo Mouse and the Scary Monster
by Louis Baum
& Sue Hellard

Let's Take Over the Nursery!
by Richard Hamilton
& Sue Heap

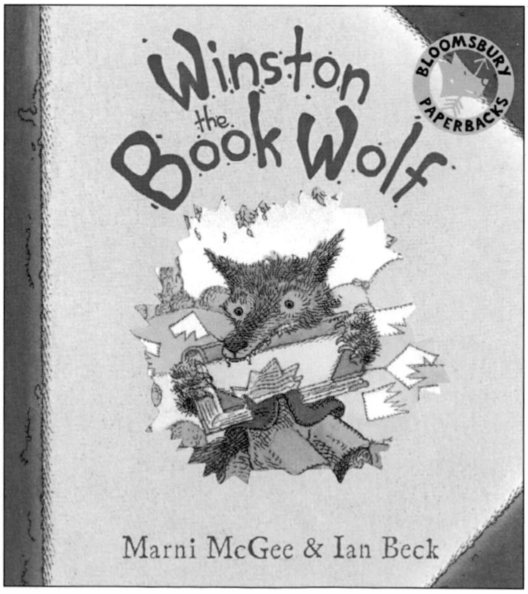

Winston the Book Wolf
by Marni McGee
& Ian Beck